WALT DISNEY'S
MICKEY MOUSE

in

SHERIFF
OF
NUGGET
GULCH

GLADSTONE PUBLISHING, LTD.
PRESCOTT, ARIZONA

Bruce Hamilton—President/Publisher	Russ Cochran—Vice President	Helen Hamilton—Treasurer
Byron Erickson—Editor-In-Chief	Leonard (John) Clark—Editor	Geoffrey Blum—Associate Editor
Gary Leach—Art Director	Susan Daigle-Leach—Production Mgr.	Virginia Gibbons—Production Asst.

Floyd Gottfredson is generally acknowledged as *the* Mickey Mouse artist, having produced the largest and most consistently readable body of comics to feature Mickey: a run of newspaper strips spanning 45 years. In that half century, he was able to lend Disney's mouse tremendous appeal by creating a series of adventures that called for intelligence, guts, and heroism. Inkers and dialogue writers on the strip came and went, but it was Gottfredson who roughed out each plot, drew the pencil art, and imbued the comic with its unique tone, a blend of toughness and good cheer.

1937 was a banner year for Gottfredson: he would wind up "Island in the Sky" and begin "Monarch of Medioka," two of the most imaginative and politically aware daily Mickey serials. Given that context, we might expect great things from "Sheriff of Nugget Gulch," but by his own admission, Gottfredson gave less time and thought to the Sunday strip, turning over the initial plotting chores to his writers. Dialogue here is loose and light, action is propelled by gag episodes rather than a continuous thread, and the main plot involving the bandit Pauncho Malarky does not even begin until halfway through the story. In what seems a woeful lack of foreshadowing, Malarky is not even mentioned until the strip of August 1, the day on which he first appears. As if to show that we are finally settling down to a serious plot, that strip ends on a cliff-hanger. Yet when we get to know Malarky, he proves to be little more than a bland copy of Peg-Leg Pete: Mickey easily tracks him down and quickly overcomes him. One suspects that Gottfredson and writer Ted Osborne did not even think up the character until well into the story.

These considerations do not make "Nugget Gulch" better or worse than the daily serials, just different. A continuous plot—even a complex one—can be spun quite nicely in short daily increments. When there is a seven-day gap in the reader's attention, however, the writer must restrict himself to basics. This is one reason that Gottfredson and Osborne shifted the setting from week to week: first to the gold fields by the river, then to the Red Nose Saloon, back to the gold fields, and finally off to the former Sheriff's front porch. The technique allowed them to move the story forward in self-contained chunks while providing an element of variety. On days when the plot offered no striking developments, a new setting or a fresh secondary character (like the droopy-mustached Sheriff) could be counted on to perk up the reader's interest. Note, for instance, how the joke of Goofy shooting off his six-guns appears two weeks in a row, with only the location changed. Perhaps Osborne believed the old showman's saying that if an audience likes something once, they'll love it twice. The repetition cannot be explained as a "running gag," one of those motifs that cartoonists use in almost musical fashion, since it never recurs again.

To figure out what makes "Nugget Gulch" tick, we have to abandon assumptions about motifs and structure. In this regard, it becomes useful to compare the story with "Sheriff of Bullet Valley," another western adventure written ten years later by Carl Barks (see **Gladstone Comic Album** 5). Both tales begin and end in roughly the same fashion, with the protagonist arriving out west and eventually being named Sheriff in recognition of his heroism. In between, however, is a world of difference. "Bullet Valley" strikes a satiric note from the first page, with a carefully honed introduction that both mocks and mourns the passing of the old frontier. "Nugget Gulch" needed no such irony: it accepts the western conventions, spinning a simple tale of good guys versus bad guys. Mickey is never less than heroic: he can be wrongfully accused, but not wrong through his own fault. It is up to Goofy to provide comedy by making mistakes or tossing off silly lines like: "It's shore purty country out here ef'n yuh like sagebrush! I don't, personally!" Donald, on the other hand, assumes the roles of both hero and clown, muddying the distinctions which "Nugget Gulch" embraces. It's a question of two wholly different authorial aims. Barks chose to play with our assumptions, while Gottfredson and Osborne adopted a more direct storytelling stance. Donald thinks through events, inviting our involvement, but Mickey *explains* them: to the simple-minded Goofy and, by extension, to the reader.

Here, then, is our clue. On Sundays Gottfredson did not so much relax his narrative standards as alter them because the stories were written for a special audience. Boys and girls who might shy clear of the more adult cartoon buried in their father's daily paper would grab at the colorful Sunday section. Atom smashers, international intrigue, and irony—the stuff of the daily strips—would have been out of place here. It was for the younger readers that Gottfredson and Osborne crafted "Nugget Gulch"—and for the kid in us all.

—**Geoffrey Blum**

Creator Credits
Front cover by Murad Gumen.

Mickey Mouse in "Sheriff of Nugget Gulch," written by Ted Osborne, penciled by Floyd Gottfredson, inked by Al Taliaferro, colored by Sue Daigle, special effects by Sue Daigle and Virginia Gibbons.

Goofy one-page gag drawn by Paul Murry, colored by Sue Daigle. (First published in *Mickey Mouse* 36, 1954.)

ISBN 0-944599-21-4

Gladstone Comic Album No. 22—Mickey Mouse in "Sheriff of Nugget Gulch"—published by Gladstone Publishing Ltd., P.O. Box 2079, Prescott, AZ 86302. Entire contents Copyright © by The Walt Disney Company. All rights reserved. Nothing herein contained may be reproduced without the written permission of The Walt Disney Company, Burbank, California.

1 3 5 7 9 8 6 4 2

HEY! GOOFY! LOOK! A LETTER FROM MINNIE!

WHAT OF IT? I GIT LETTERS ALL THUH TIME -- AN' YUH DON'T SEE ME GETTIN' SO HET UP ABOUT 'EM!

BUT LOOK! SHE SAYS GOLD HAS BEEN DISCOVERED IN NUGGET GULCH! MINERS ARE FLOCKIN' IN! EVERY-BODY'S GETTIN' RICH! JUST LIKE TH' DAYS O' '49!

49 WHAT?

LISTEN, GOOFY! WE'RE GOIN' OUT THERE! IT'S TH' CHANCE OF A LIFETIME! WE'RE LEAVIN' ON TH' NEXT TRAIN! HOW FAST CAN YOU PACK?

GOIN' OUT WEST? GAWSH, MICKEY— I'M PACKED NOW!

OKAY! HERE'S SOME MONEY! GET YOURSELF SOME WESTERN CLOTHES AN' I'LL MEET YOU AT THE STATION IN TWO HOURS!

AND SO, TWO HOURS LATER --

HERE I AM, MICKEY! HOW DO I LOOK?

SWELL, GOOFY! YOU LOOK LIKE A REGULAR TWO-GUN MAN!

SHERIFF OF NUGGET GULCH

MICKEY MOUSE

THIS IS A HECK OF A WAY T' BE GOIN' OUT WEST—LIKE A COUPLE O' CONVICTS!

SHUCKS, MICKEY— I DIDN'T THINK NOBODY'D MIND! I THOUGHT THEY'D BE USED TO IT!

WELL—WE'RE HERE! I'VE TURNED YOUR BAGGAGE OVER TO THE SHERIFF!

THE SHERIFF?

YEAH! HE'S COMIN' ABOARD NOW! I WIRED AHEAD FOR HIM TO MEET THE TRAIN!

HERE THEY ARE, SHERIFF! THEY SHOT UP THE TRAIN SOMETHING AWFUL!

ALL RIGHT! GIT ALONG WITH YUH! BUT ONE FALSE MOVE AN' I'LL PLUG YUH!

THEY'RE THE ONES! THEY SHOT UP A TRAIN IN BROAD DAYLIGHT!

THE TOUGHEST DESPERADOES SINCE THE DALTON GANG!

—FASTER ON THE TRIGGER THAN BILL HICKOCK!

—EITHER ONE OF 'EM WOULD SHOOT YOU QUICKER'N SCAT!

GAWSH, MICKEY! WE'RE FAMOUS!

LIVERY FEED

THE RED DOG

GENERAL STORE

BANK

HOTEL

SHERIFF OF NUGGET GULCH

SHERIFF OF NUGGET GULCH

MICKEY MOUSE

SHERIFF OF NUGGET GULCH

BOO!

HAW! HAW! HAW! HAW! LOOK AT 'EM GO! BOY! HAVE I GOT 'EM BUFFALOED?

BANG!! BANG!! BANG!

FER GOSH SAKES! WHAT'S THAT? SHOOTIN'?

YES! THE BOYS HAVE BEEN TARGET-PRACTICING EVER SINCE THEY HEARD YOU WERE COMING TO TOWN!

WELL, THEY OUGHTA BE MORE CAREFUL! SOME O' THOSE SHOTS SOUNDED PRETTY CLOSE TO US!

HEY! MICKEY! LOOK! I NEVER NOTICED ALL THESE MOTH-HOLES BEFORE!

MOTH-HOLES! YOU BIG SAP, THOSE ARE BULLET-HOLES!

WELL I'LL BE DURNED!

KIN YUH IMAGINE A GUY, SELLIN' ME A HAT FULL O' BULLET-HOLES? IF IT WASN'T SO FUR I'D GO BACK AN' MAKE 'IM EXCHANGE IT!

SHERIFF OF NUGGET GULCH

MICKEY MOUSE

SHERIFF OF NUGGET GULCH

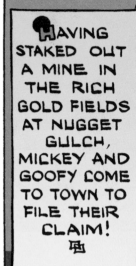

SHERIFF OF NUGGET GULCH

NOW YOU'VE DONE IT, YOU BIG DUMMY! TH' WHOLE TOWN WILL BE AFTER YOU FOR THIS! WHAT HAPPENED?

GAWSH, MICKEY! I CAN'T FIGGER IT OUT!

I WENT IN AN' EVERYBODY WAS HID, SO I SHOT A COUPLA TIMES UP IN THUH AIR TO ATTRACT ATTENTION!

YEAH! YOU JUST SHOT UP IN THE AIR! I SEE!

WELL, FUST THING I KNEW, ALL THESE TOUGH GUYS WAS THERE, WATCHIN' ME! I WANTED TUH SHOW 'EM HOW TOUGH I WAS -- SO I BANGED ON THUH BAR AN' ORDERED!

YOU MEAN -- YOU DIDN'T SHOOT 'EM?

O'COURSE NOT!

WELL--- WHAT DID YOU ORDER?

I JEST SAYS: "GIMME A SARS'PARILLA--- STRAIGHT!"

AN' WHEN I LOOKED AROUND, THEY'D ALL PASSED OUT!

FUR GAWSH SAKES, WHAT YUH LAUGHIN' AT?

TH' TOUGHEST MAN SINCE WILD BILL HICKOK! HO HO HO HO HO HO!

MICKEY MOUSE

SHERIFF OF NUGGET GULCH

SHERIFF OF NUGGET GULCH

MICKEY MOUSE

SHERIFF OF NUGGET GULCH

THUH ONLY TIME YUH NEED TUH LOOK UP A FELLER'S RECORD IS WHEN YUH WANT SOMETHIN' PURTY TO CARVE ON HIS TOMBSTONE!

SHOOTIN' SHERIFFS IS ONE O' THIS TOWN'S MOST POP'LAR SPORTS! AN' THUH BIGGER YER REPUTATION THUH MORE FUN IT IS TUH TRY TUH PLUG YUH!

WELL-- HAVE YOU GOT ANY SPECIAL ADVICE FOR ME?

NOPE! JEST KEEP YER EYES PEELED AN' YER GUN HANDY! AN' WHEN ANYTHING HAPPENS, GIT INTO ACTION QUICK!

GOOD-BYE, SON--AN' GOOD LUCK! TAKE KEER O' YERSELF!

THANK YOU, SIR! I'LL SURE DO MY BEST!

THAT'S WHY I THINK YER GONNA MAKE A DURNED GOOD SHERIFF!

YOU MEAN--BECAUSE I'M GONNA TRY HARD?

NOPE! BECAUSE EVERY GUNMAN IN TOWN IS GONNA TAKE A CRACK AT YUH--

---AN YER SO LITTLE, YER GONNA BE HARD TUH HIT!

SHERIFF OF NUGGET GULCH

MICKEY MOUSE

SHERIFF OF NUGGET GULCH

MICKEY MOUSE

SHERIFF OF NUGGET GULCH

TRY T' HOLD US UP, WILL YA? I'LL SHOW YOU WHAT WE DO TO-----

FUR GAWRSH SAKES! WHADDA I DO NOW?

MICKEY MOUSE

SHERIFF OF NUGGET GULCH

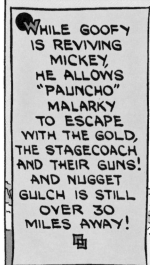

SHERIFF OF NUGGET GULCH

MICKEY MOUSE

SHERIFF OF NUGGET GULCH

MICKEY MOUSE

SHERIFF OF NUGGET GULCH

MICKEY MOUSE

SHERIFF OF NUGGET GULCH

MICKEY MOUSE

SHERIFF OF NUGGET GULCH

SHERIFF OF NUGGET GULCH

MICKEY MOUSE

MICKEY MOUSE

THE MINERS' GOLD HAS BEEN RETURNED, PAUNCHO MALARKY IS IN JAIL, AND MICKEY IS THE HERO OF NUGGET GULCH!

MICKEY, WE MINERS AN' VIGILANTES WANTED TUH DO SOMETHIN' TUH THANK YUH FUR WHAT YUH DONE FUR US!

AW, SHUCKS! I JUST DID MY JOB!

THAT'S JEST IT! YUH DONE SUCH A GOOD JOB THAT WE DECIDED TUH MAKE YUH OUR SHERIFF FUR THUH REST O' YER LIFE! HERE'S YER STAR!

THAT'S SURE NICE OF YOU! BUT--BUT I CAN'T TAKE IT!

WHY NOT? IT'S SOLID GOLD!

WELL, YOU SEE I'M NOT GOIN' TO STAY HERE! MINNIE AN' GOOFY AN' I ARE LEAVIN' FOR HOME-- RIGHT AWAY!

THAT MAKES NO DIFFERENCE!

WHEREVER YUH GO, YUH'RE STILL SHERIFF O' NUGGET GULCH! WHOEVER TAKES YER PLACE IS JEST GONNA BE A DEPUTY!

WE'LL HOLD YER JOB OPEN-- AN' WHENEVER YUH WANT TUH COME BACK, YUH STEP RIGHT INTO OFFICE!

GOSH! IF THAT'S TH' WAY YOU FEEL, I'LL SURE WEAR IT!

SHERIFF OF NUGGET GULCH

BUT I'VE GOT T' BE SAYIN' GOOD-BYE, NOW! MINNIE AN' GOOFY ARE PROB'LY WAITIN' OUT IN TH' STAGECOACH!

YUH CAN'T SAY GOOD-BYE TUH ME YIT, YOUNG FELLER! I'M RIDIN' DOWN TO THUH TRAIN WITH YUH!

AND SO---MICKEY AND HIS GANG LEAVE THE LITTLE MINING TOWN--AND RIDE ACROSS THE DESERT TO THE TRAIN!

NUGGET GULCH IS SORRY TUH LOSE YUH, MICKEY! YUH'RE THUH BEST SHERIFF WE EVER HAD IN THESE PARTS!

EXPRESS

SO LONG, CHIEF!

G'BYE! AN' EF'N WE EVER GIT ANOTHER MESS O' BANDITS, WE'RE GONNA SEND FUR YUH TUH COME BACK AN' CLEAN 'EM OUT!

AN'--WHO KNOWS?-- MEBBE SOME DAY I'LL **DO** IT!

EXPRESS